W9-ARV-489

Searchlight BOOKS™

What Do You
Know about
Maps?

Using

Climate Maps

Rebecca E. Hirsch

Lerner Publications ◆ Minneapolis

Lerner Publications Company
A division of Lerner Publishing Group, Inc.
241 First Avenue North
Minneapolis, MN 55401 USA

For reading levels and more information, look up this title
at www.lernerbooks.com.

Library of Congress Cataloging-in-Publication Data

Names: Hirsch, Rebecca E., author.
Title: Using climate maps / Rebecca E. Hirsch.
Description: Minneapolis : Lerner Publications, [2017] | Series: Searchlight Books. What Do You Know about Maps? | Includes bibliographical references and index.
Identifiers: LCCN 2015044351 (print) | LCCN 2016001199 (ebook) | ISBN 9781512409505 (lb : alk. paper) | ISBN 9781512412918 (pb : alk. paper) | ISBN 9781512410709 (eb pdf)
Subjects: LCSH: Maps—Juvenile literature. | Weather—Maps—Juvenile literature.
Classification: LCC GA105.6 .H57 2017 (print) | LCC GA105.6 (ebook) | DDC 912.01/4—dc23

LC record available at http://lccn.loc.gov/2015044351

Manufactured in the United States of America
1-39539-21243-3/15/2016

Contents

Chapter 1

WHAT IS A CLIMATE MAP?

Imagine you want to plant a garden. You want your garden in a spot that is warm and sunny. You have a map that shows you the conditions in your yard. The map shows that the area under the tree is cool and shady. It shows you that a spot near the back door is sunny. Now you know where to plant your garden.

A climate map can help you choose a spot to plant a garden. What kind of information does a climate map show?

A map is a diagram that represents a place. The place shown on a map may be big, like the whole world, or small, like a backyard. Maps can show different kinds of information about a place. Some maps show the natural features of a place, such as mountains, rivers, and forests. Some maps show information about the climate, like the map of the yard. These are called climate maps.

This map shows different climates in the lower forty-eight US states.

A climate map can show the temperature of a certain place. It could show how much, if any, snow falls. These are some important features of climate. Other climate features are fog, humidity, and the strength and speed of the wind.

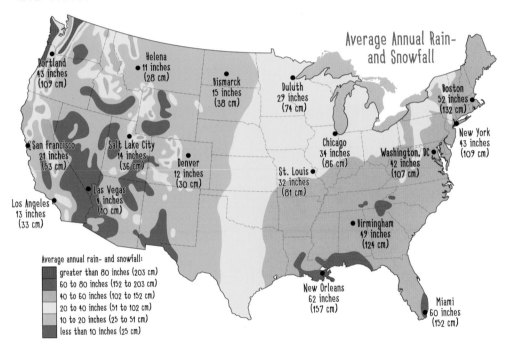

Average Annual Rain- and Snowfall

Portland
43 inches
(109 cm)

Helena
11 inches
(28 cm)

Bismarck
15 inches
(38 cm)

Duluth
29 inches
(74 cm)

Boston
52 inches
(132 cm)

New York
43 inches
(109 cm)

San Francisco
21 inches
(53 cm)

Salt Lake City
14 inches
(36 cm)

Denver
12 inches
(30 cm)

Chicago
34 inches
(86 cm)

Washington, DC
42 inches
(107 cm)

St. Louis
32 inches
(81 cm)

Las Vegas
4 inches
(10 cm)

Los Angeles
13 inches
(33 cm)

Birmingham
49 inches
(124 cm)

Average annual rain- and snowfall:
greater than 80 inches (203 cm)
60 to 80 inches (152 to 203 cm)
40 to 60 inches (102 to 152 cm)
20 to 40 inches (51 to 102 cm)
10 to 20 inches (25 to 51 cm)
less than 10 inches (25 cm)

New Orleans
62 inches
(157 cm)

Miami
60 inches
(152 cm)

On this map, you can see the average yearly amount of rain and snow in different parts of the United States.

Climate vs. Weather

A climate map doesn't show the weather. Weather refers to short-term conditions, like whether it is raining or sunny outside. Weather can change from hour to hour or day to day. Climate is the usual weather in a place. Climate doesn't change from day to day. A climate map shows the average conditions that have taken place over many years.

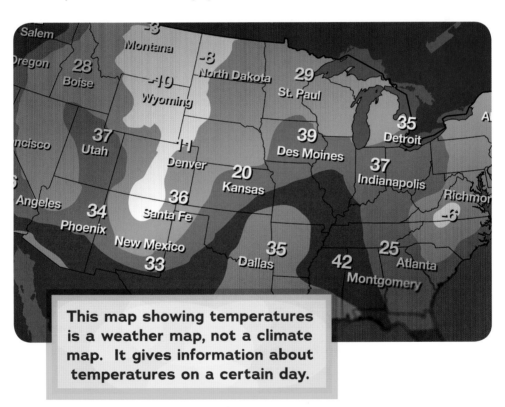

This map showing temperatures is a weather map, not a climate map. It gives information about temperatures on a certain day.

What Climate Maps Show

A climate map may show a small region, such as a town. Or it may show different climates around the world. Some parts of the world are hot and rainy. They have a tropical, wet climate. Others are cold and snowy. They have a polar climate. In between are many other climates. Any kind of climate might appear on a climate map.

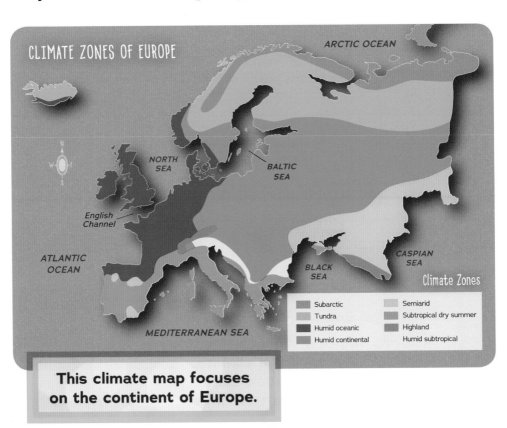

CLIMATE ZONES OF EUROPE

ARCTIC OCEAN

NORTH SEA

BALTIC SEA

English Channel

ATLANTIC OCEAN

BLACK SEA

CASPIAN SEA

MEDITERRANEAN SEA

Climate Zones

- Subarctic
- Tundra
- Humid oceanic
- Humid continental
- Semiarid
- Subtropical dry summer
- Highland
- Humid subtropical

This climate map focuses on the continent of Europe.

No single map can show everything. So cartographers (people who make maps) choose which features to show. They include only the features that will help people using the map.

A climate map usually shows one type of climate condition. It might show the amount of rain an area receives or the percentage of cloudy days. A single map won't show all the climate conditions.

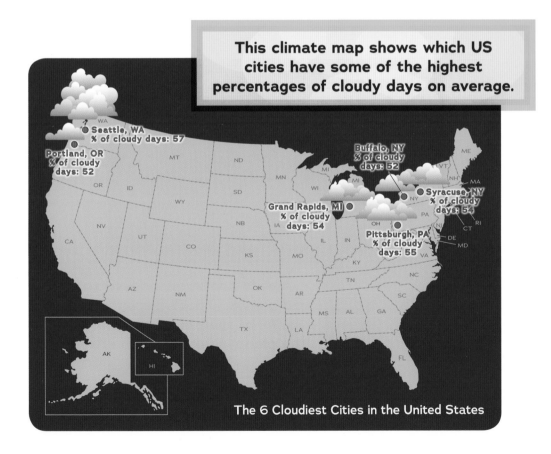

This climate map shows which US cities have some of the highest percentages of cloudy days on average.

Seattle, WA
% of cloudy days: 57

Portland, OR
% of cloudy days: 52

Buffalo, NY
% of cloudy days: 52

Syracuse, NY
% of cloudy days: 54

Grand Rapids, MI
% of cloudy days: 54

Pittsburgh, PA
% of cloudy days: 55

The 6 Cloudiest Cities in the United States

Mapping the Climate of Mars

Scientists have mapped the climate on Mars. They have created maps showing different temperatures. Mars is much colder than Earth. The average temperature on Mars is about –80°F (–62°C). Scientists have also mapped storms on Mars. Dust storms can grow to cover the whole planet. These giant storms can last for months.

Mars is sometimes called the red planet. That's because iron oxide, or rust, in its soil makes the planet look red from space.

Chapter 2

WHAT'S ON A CLIMATE MAP?

Climate maps can give you a great deal of information if you know how to read them. Maps use a special language of symbols. These symbols include colors, words, and lines. A legend is a key that will help you read the map. The legend explains the meaning of the symbols used on the map.

Temperature Ranges:

- 32 to 40°F (0 to 4°C)
- 40 to 50°F (4 to 10°C)
- 50 to 60°F (10 to 16°C)
- 60 to 70°F (16 to 21°C)
- 70 to 80°F (21 to 27°C)
- 80 to 90°F (27 to 32°C)
- over 90°F (32°C)

This legend shows the meaning of different colors on a map. What is a legend?

Climate maps often share certain features. Many climate maps have a title. The title tells you what information the map shows and what place it represents. Climate maps may have a compass rose that shows direction. It tells which way on the map are north, south, east, and west.

This compass rose is labeled with letters for each of the four directions.

Scale

Climate maps might include a scale so you can estimate distances. All climate maps are smaller than the actual places they represent. A scale explains the relationship between distances on the map and distances in the real world. Maps may use different kinds of scales. The most common kind looks like a ruler.

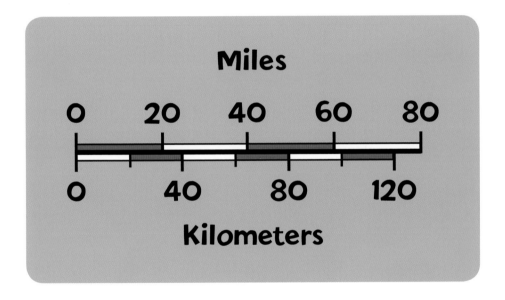

SCALES LIKE THIS ONE ARE OFTEN
NEAR THE BOTTOM OF A CLIMATE MAP.

Colors

Color is an important symbol on a climate map. Cartographers use color or shading to show different climate features. Mapmakers choose what feature they want to emphasize. A climate map may show precipitation (rainfall or snowfall), temperature, humidity, sunshine, or another weather feature.

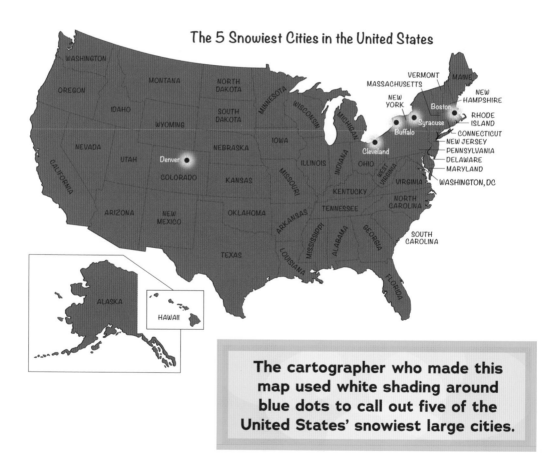

The 5 Snowiest Cities in the United States

The cartographer who made this map used white shading around blue dots to call out five of the United States' snowiest large cities.

Precipitation is a very common thing to show on a climate map. Most maps that show precipitation reflect the average precipitation levels recorded over months or years. Using information collected over a long period of time makes the map more accurate.

Buffalo, New York (ABOVE), is considered one of the snowiest US cities because it has some of the highest snow levels recorded over many years.

A temperature map is another kind of climate map. On a temperature map, colors show how warm or cold a place usually is. Red may stand for warmer weather. Blue may stand for colder weather. As with precipitation, the temperature shown is the average over one month, an entire year, or longer.

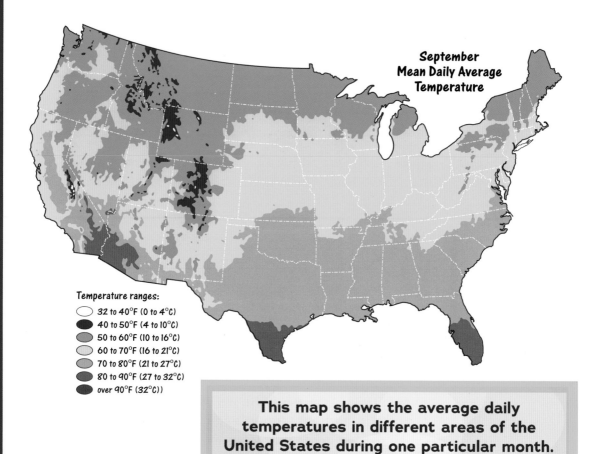

September Mean Daily Average Temperature

Temperature ranges:

- 32 to 40°F (0 to 4°C)
- 40 to 50°F (4 to 10°C)
- 50 to 60°F (10 to 16°C)
- 60 to 70°F (16 to 21°C)
- 70 to 80°F (21 to 27°C)
- 80 to 90°F (27 to 32°C)
- over 90°F (32°C)

This map shows the average daily temperatures in different areas of the United States during one particular month.

Latitude and Climate

Climate maps often have lines called latitude lines. These imaginary lines run from east to west around the globe. The middle latitude line is the equator. It divides the globe into two halves: the Northern Hemisphere and the Southern Hemisphere. Above the equator, more latitude lines continue to the top of the world, the North Pole. Below the equator, they continue to the bottom of the world, the South Pole.

Many different kinds of maps have latitude lines. Can you find the equator on this map?

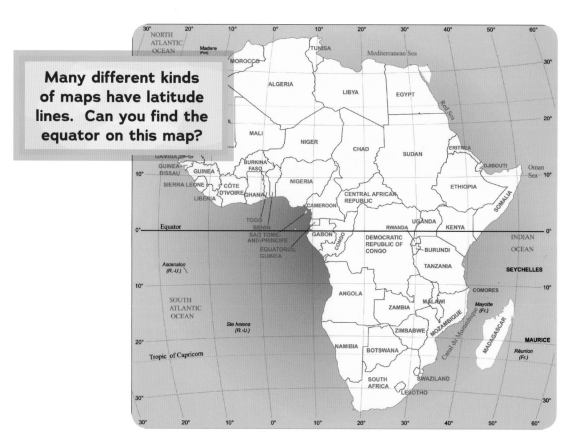

Latitude has a big effect on climate. If you look at a climate map of the world, you can see a pattern. The tropics is a hot region near the equator. As you go farther from the equator, it gets colder. The North Pole and South Pole, which are farthest from the equator, are very cold.

THE SOUTH POLE IS VERY CHILLY!

The Father of Geography

Eratosthenes, an ancient Greek scholar, divided Earth into five climatic regions: two freezing zones around the North Pole and the South Pole, two temperate (mild) zones, and a hot zone near the equator. He was the first person to use the word *geography*.

Eratosthenes lived from about 276 to 195 BCE.

Seasons

Seasons influence climate. Seasons happen as Earth circles around the sun. This trip takes one full year. Meanwhile, Earth also rotates, or spins, on its axis. The axis is tilted. This rotation gives rise to day and night.

Earth's trip around the sun helps give rise to seasons. The beginning of fall is called the fall equinox.

The trip around the sun and Earth's tilt work together to create seasons. In different seasons, places on Earth receive different amounts and strengths of sunlight. When the Northern Hemisphere is tilted away from the sun, it experiences winter. Meanwhile, the Southern Hemisphere is tilted toward the sun. It experiences summer.

Seasons can have a big effect on climate. To see how, look at a climate map of one place at different times of the year.

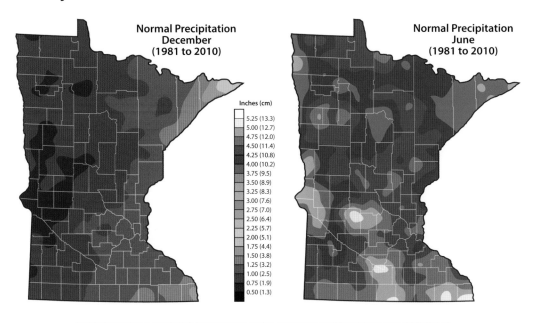

Normal Precipitation
December
(1981 to 2010)

Normal Precipitation
June
(1981 to 2010)

Inches (cm)
5.25 (13.3)
5.00 (12.7)
4.75 (12.0)
4.50 (11.4)
4.25 (10.8)
4.00 (10.2)
3.75 (9.5)
3.50 (8.9)
3.25 (8.3)
3.00 (7.6)
2.75 (7.0)
2.50 (6.4)
2.25 (5.7)
2.00 (5.1)
1.75 (4.4)
1.50 (3.8)
1.25 (3.2)
1.00 (2.5)
0.75 (1.9)
0.50 (1.3)

The map on the left shows precipitation in Minnesota in December from 1981 to 2010. The map on the right shows precipitation in Minnesota in June from 1981 to 2010.

Climate Zones

Scientists sort climates into five major groups, called climate zones. These zones are based on average temperature and precipitation. The climate zones are tropical, dry, mild, continental, and polar. Many scientists add a sixth zone for mountain climates. Each zone can be further divided into smaller, more descriptive groups. These zones and groups often go by different names on different maps. For example, very dry climates can be called dry, arid, or desert.

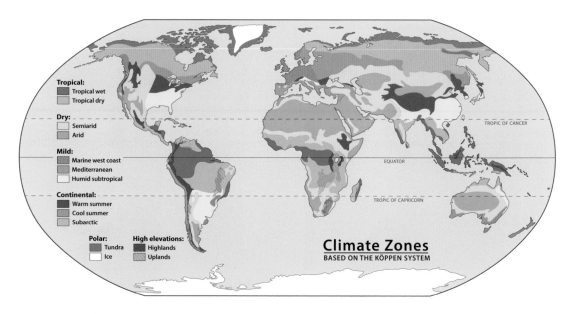

Tropical:
- Tropical wet
- Tropical dry

Dry:
- Semiarid
- Arid

Mild:
- Marine west coast
- Mediterranean
- Humid subtropical

Continental:
- Warm summer
- Cool summer
- Subarctic

Polar:
- Tundra
- Ice

High elevations:
- Highlands
- Uplands

TROPIC OF CANCER

EQUATOR

TROPIC OF CAPRICORN

Climate Zones
BASED ON THE KÖPPEN SYSTEM

This map shows six climate zones and the smaller groups into which they are sometimes divided.

A tropical climate is warm and rainy. Tropical climates are found near the equator. Hawaii is a place with a tropical climate.

A dry climate receives very little rain or snow. This type of climate is usually hot. Phoenix, Arizona, is a city with a dry climate.

Hawaii's warm climate makes it a popular vacation spot.

A mild climate has hot, dry summers and cool, rainy winters. This climate is often found near an ocean. Los Angeles has a mild climate. Different types of mild climates include Mediterranean and oceanic.

A continental climate occurs in the center of a continent. Iowa has a continental climate. Summers are warm or hot. Winters are cold. A continental climate is one of the few climate zones with four distinct seasons: winter, spring, summer, and fall.

Places with mild and continental climates are sometimes called temperate regions.

Leaves turn beautiful colors in the fall in a continental climate.

A polar climate is cold. Polar climates are near the North Pole and the South Pole. Some polar regions, such as northern Alaska, have a short, chilly summer. Other regions, such as Antarctica, remain extremely cold even in summer. A mountain peak may also have a polar climate.

Antarctica is known for its year-round snow and ice cover.

Chapter 3

HOW DO YOU USE A CLIMATE MAP?

A climate map can help you learn about different cultures. The clothing people wear is influenced by climate. People in Greenland wear warm clothing to survive their chilly climate. Climate also can help you understand what kind of food people eat. Some native peoples of Canada, Greenland, Alaska, and Siberia depend on animals for food because few plants grow in polar regions.

People in Greenland must bundle up! How can climate maps help you learn about different cultures?

26

Climate maps can tell you about life in different states too. For instance, Florida is usually hot and muggy. Oregon is often cool and foggy. Looking at a climate map can help you understand how people in different states dress, what sports and outdoor activities they might take part in, and what crops they grow.

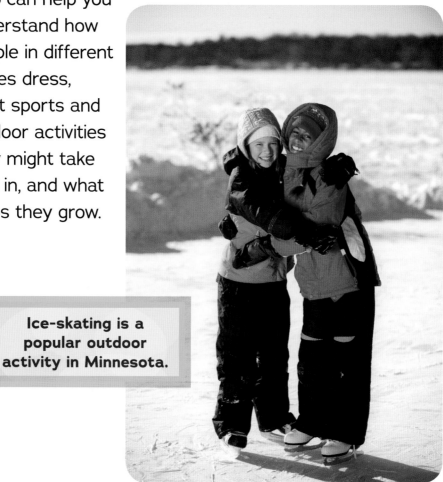

Ice-skating is a popular outdoor activity in Minnesota.

Climate maps can tell you about a region's plant and animal life. Different kinds of vegetation grow in different climates. Lush rain forests grow in areas with tropical climates. Polar climates have no trees. The plants and animals that live in dry climates are adapted to the lack of rain.

A CACTUS IS A STURDY PLANT THAT CAN SURVIVE WITH LITTLE WATER.

Microclimates

Sometimes the climate of one area differs from the surrounding area. This is known as a microclimate. Cities and lakes can cause microclimates. A city is often warmer than its surroundings. This happens because streets and buildings absorb heat from the sun. Lakes influence climate when cold winds blow across warm lake water and pick up moisture. Cities on the southern side of Lake Ontario receive much more snow than cities on the northern side.

Snowfall caused by moisture from a lake is called lake-effect snow.

Gardening

Gardeners often use climate maps. Certain plants grow best in certain kinds of weather. For instance, tomatoes grow best in warm weather. Peas grow better in cool weather. A gardener can check a climate map to decide the best season to plant.

A plant hardiness map is a special type of climate map. It shows different zones based on the average minimum winter temperature. Colder zones are shown in purple. Warmer zones are shown in red. Certain plants grow better in colder or warmer zones. Gardeners can check a climate map to see if a specific plant can survive in their area.

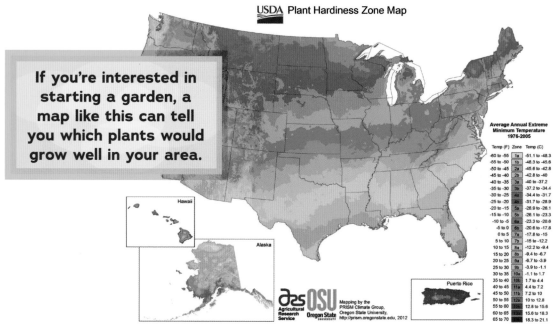

USDA Plant Hardiness Zone Map

If you're interested in starting a garden, a map like this can tell you which plants would grow well in your area.

Average Annual Extreme Minimum Temperature 1976-2005

Temp (F)	Zone	Temp (C)
-60 to -55	1a	-51.1 to -48.3
-55 to -50	1b	-48.3 to -45.6
-50 to -45	2a	-45.6 to -42.8
-45 to -40	2b	-42.8 to -40
-40 to -35	3a	-40 to -37.2
-35 to -30	3b	-37.2 to -34.4
-30 to -25	4a	-34.4 to -31.7
-25 to -20	4b	-31.7 to -28.9
-20 to -15	5a	-28.9 to -26.1
-15 to -10	5b	-26.1 to -23.3
-10 to -5	6a	-23.3 to -20.6
-5 to 0	6b	-20.6 to -17.8
0 to 5	7a	-17.8 to -15
5 to 10	7b	-15 to -12.2
10 to 15	8a	-12.2 to -9.4
15 to 20	8b	-9.4 to -6.7
20 to 25	9a	-6.7 to -3.9
25 to 30	9b	-3.9 to -1.1
30 to 35	10a	-1.1 to 1.7
35 to 40	10b	1.7 to 4.4
40 to 45	11a	4.4 to 7.2
45 to 50	11b	7.2 to 10
50 to 55	12a	10 to 12.8
55 to 60	12b	12.8 to 15.6
60 to 65	13a	15.6 to 18.3
65 to 70	13b	18.3 to 21.1

Hawaii

Alaska

Puerto Rico

Agricultural Research Service

OSU Oregon State UNIVERSITY

Mapping by the PRISM Climate Group, Oregon State University, http://prism.oregonstate.edu, 2012

Climate Change

Climate is always changing. Most climate changes happen slowly over thousands of years. There have been cold periods in the past, when the climate was colder than it is today. During periods called ice ages, huge sheets of ice covered large portions of Earth. During the last ice age, ice sheets covered much of Canada and extended into the United States. Climate maps can help you understand these changes.

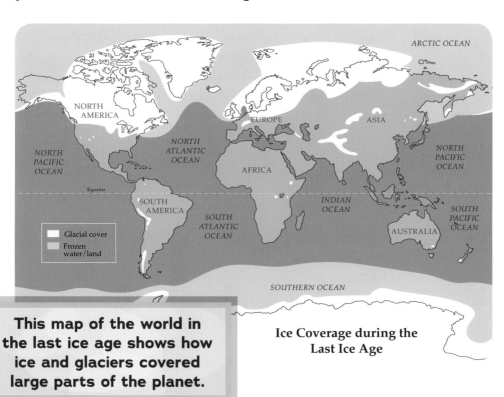

This map of the world in the last ice age shows how ice and glaciers covered large parts of the planet.

Ice Coverage during the Last Ice Age

At other times in the past, the climate has been warmer. In the twenty-first century, Earth's climate is growing warmer faster than in the past. This is called global warming. It is caused by air pollution. Global warming is melting polar ice and changing weather conditions around the world. It is changing where people can live and grow crops. Scientists use climate maps to track and study these changes.

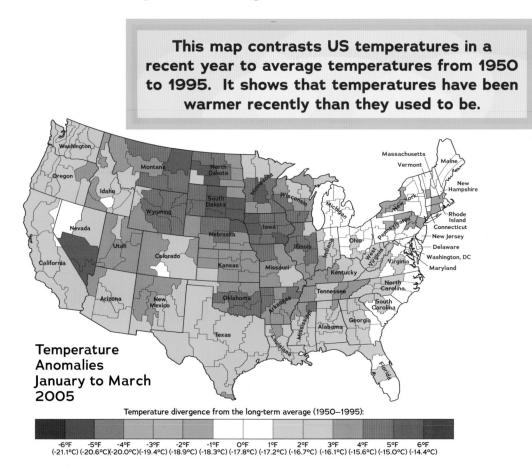

This map contrasts US temperatures in a recent year to average temperatures from 1950 to 1995. It shows that temperatures have been warmer recently than they used to be.

Temperature Anomalies January to March 2005

Temperature divergence from the long-term average (1950–1995):

| -6°F | -5°F | -4°F | -3°F | -2°F | -1°F | 0°F | 1°F | 2°F | 3°F | 4°F | 5°F | 6°F |
| (-21.1°C) | (-20.6°C) | (-20.0°C) | (-19.4°C) | (-18.9°C) | (-18.3°C) | (-17.8°C) | (-17.2°C) | (-16.7°C) | (-16.1°C) | (-15.6°C) | (-15.0°C) | (-14.4°C) |

Did You Know?

Climate maps help scientists understand global warming. Scientists measure temperature, precipitation, and many other climate features around the world. They create maps to see how the climate is changing. They can learn what places and people are most affected.

Hurricane Katrina was a huge storm that hit New Orleans in 2005. Climate change could make strong storms like this more likely.

Chapter 4

ARE YOU A CLIMATE MAP WHIZ?

Test your map smarts! Say you live in Iowa. Your class is planting a garden. You live in the middle of Iowa. This map shows Iowa planting zones. Can you find your area's average minimum temperature?

USDA Plant Hardiness Zone Map
Iowa

Average Annual Extreme Minimum Temperature 1976-2005

Temp (F)	Zone	Temp (C)
-25 to -20	4b	-31.7 to -28.9
-20 to -15	5a	-28.9 to -26.1
-15 to -10	5b	-26.1 to -23.3
-10 to -5	6a	-23.3 to -20.6

In what zone is central Iowa?

Your class decides to plant tomatoes and peppers. You must consider when to plant your garden, because these plants cannot survive freezing temperatures. This map shows the date of the last spring freeze for the state. What is the last spring freeze date in your area? When would be a good time to plant your garden?

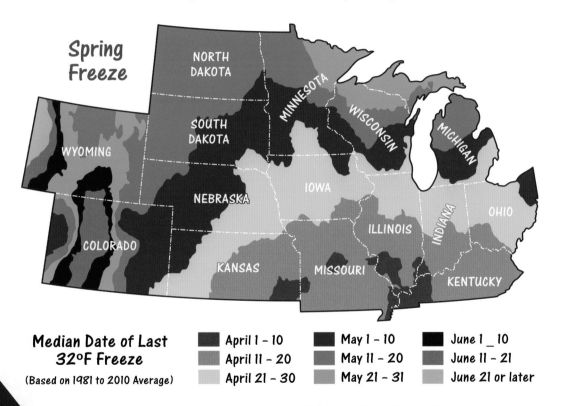

Spring Freeze

Median Date of Last 32°F Freeze

(Based on 1981 to 2010 Average)

April 1 – 10	May 1 – 10	June 1 _ 10
April 11 – 20	May 11 – 20	June 11 – 21
April 21 – 30	May 21 – 31	June 21 or later

Median date is determined such that half of all years fall before and half fall after the median date.

Now pretend you live in far northern Wisconsin. What is the last spring freeze date there?

You Did It!

Congratulations on a job well done! You have learned all about climate maps. These maps give you information about temperature, precipitation, and other climate features. They can help you understand what kinds of animals and plants live and grow in a place and how people have adapted to that place. Climate maps help you learn how climate has changed over time. Learning about the climate of a place will help you understand more about that place and how it relates to the world.

It's fun to learn about the world through maps!

Fun Facts

- Death Valley in the Mojave Desert is the hottest spot on the planet. The temperature once hit 134°F (57°C).

- Of all the climates on Earth, Antarctica's dry valleys are the most like the conditions on Mars. Scientists come to the dry valleys to study what the climate on Mars is like.

- Rainfall is low in all dry climates, but one of the driest places is the Atacama Desert in Chile. There is so little rain that villagers use fine mesh nets to collect moisture from fog. The water drips into troughs, and pipes carry it to the village.

Glossary

adapted: changed so as to be able to live or grow in a specific place

cartographer: a person who makes maps

compass rose: a circle showing the directions of north, south, east, and west on a map

continental: a climate type with hot or mild summers and cold winters, usually found in the interior of a continent

global warming: a warming of Earth's atmosphere and oceans that is caused by specific kinds of air pollution

humidity: the amount of moisture in the air

ice age: a time in the past when ice sheets were widespread on Earth's surface

latitude: a distance north or south of the equator measured in degrees

legend: an explanatory list of symbols on a map

polar: a type of cold climate found around the North Pole and the South Pole

precipitation: water that falls to the earth as hail, mist, rain, sleet, or snow

scale: a tool that explains the size of a map compared to the actual place it represents

temperate: having a climate that is usually mild without extremely cold or extremely hot temperatures

tropical: having a warm, moist climate as in the tropics, a region found near the equator

vegetation: the plant life of an area

Learn More about Climate Maps

Books

Cole, Joanna. *The Magic School Bus and the Climate Challenge*. New York: Scholastic Press, 2010. This book delivers an action-packed adventure to help you learn why Earth is getting warmer and what people can do about it.

Reilly, Kathleen M. *Explore Weather and Climate! With 25 Great Projects*. White River Junction, Vermont: Nomad Press, 2012. Explore the world of weather and climate with hands-on projects and interesting facts.

Rowell, Rebecca. *Weather and Climate through Infographics*. Minneapolis: Lerner Publications, 2014. Check out this book for charts, maps, and illustrations that help you make sense of weather and climate.

Websites

NASA: Weather and Climate
http://climatekids.nasa.gov/menu/weather-and-climate
Stop by this fun site for activities, games, photos, and answers to your tricky questions about weather and climate.

NOAA: Climate Zones
http://oceanservice.noaa.gov/education/pd/oceans_weather_climate/media/climate_zones.swf
Explore an interactive map showing the climate zones of the world.

USDA Plant Hardiness Zone Map
http://planthardiness.ars.usda.gov/PHZMWeb
On this site, you can view a map of the entire country showing gardening zones or select your state to see a detailed state map.

LERNER

SOURCE

Expand learning beyond the printed book. Download free, complementary educational resources for this book from our website, www.lernerresource.com.

Index

Photo Acknowledgments

The images in this book are used with the permission of: © iStockphoto.com/Michael Luhrenberg, p. 4; © Laura Westlund/Independent Picture Service, pp. 5, 6, 8, 9, 11, 13, 14, 16, 21, 22, 31, 32, 35; © iStockphoto.com/SpiffyJ, p. 7; © Science Source, p. 10; © Julynx/Dreamstime.com, p. 12; © Mike Groll/Stringery/Getty Images, p. 15; © Martine Oger/Dreamstime.com, p. 17; © Dmytro Pylypenko/Shutterstock.com, p. 18; © INTERFOTO/Alamy, p. 19; © Damon Yancy/Dreamstime.com, p. 20; © iStockphoto.com/global_explorer, p. 23; © iStockphoto.com/LawrenceSawyer, p. 24; © Steve Allen/Dreamstime.com, p. 25; © M. Lohmann/picture alliance/blickwinkel/M/Newscom, p. 26; © iStockphoto.com/Christopher Futcher, pp. 27, 36; © iStockphoto.com/MotoEd, p. 28; © Verevkin/Dreamstime.com, p. 29; Agricultural Research Service, USDA, pp. 30, 34; Courtesy of the National Oceanic and Atmospheric Administration Central Library Photo Collection, p. 33.

Front cover: © Laura Westlund/Independent Picture Service (map); © iStockphoto.com/Devaev Dmitriy (background).

Main body text set in Adrianna Regular 14/20.
Typeface provided by Chank.